For Bronx.

Once there was a dog who wanted to play,
She sat in the garden and waited all day.
She looked through the fence and looked
through the gate,
hoping someone might pass and be her
mate.

She sat and she waited until the break of day,
in the hope that someone might come and play.
But no-one came, so she lay down and thought,
then all of a sudden, jumped up with a start.

She had a plan to escape the yard.
It was now her mission, even though it was hard.
She climbed the fence, she didn't care about her
owners wrath
and she trundled off along the path.

Over grass and fields she walked,
past groups of people who just talked and talked.
She padded through a cobbled town
and noticed people walking in caps and gowns

People drank coffee, sat on chairs on the street,
as she maneuvered around hundreds of feet.
She heard bells ring and followed the sound,
until she came to some steps that went around and
around.

She followed 350 steps all the way to the top.
She was so high that her ears popped.
When she eventually got to the top,
she was so tired she lay herself down on the ground
with a big *FLOP.*

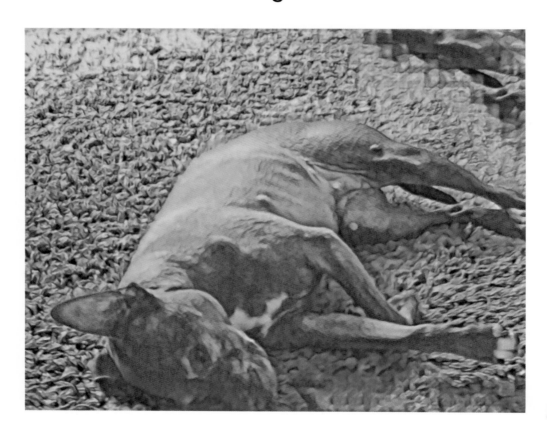

After a short rest she continued her adventure
and ended up at the Prince Bishops shopping
Centre.
She walked until she came to a stop
and looked inside the Discovering Durham shop.

Next she walked to a coffee shop where she saw a plate
and on that plate some delicious leftover carrot cake.
She gobbled up the cake then started to think,
I am very thirsty, now I need to find a drink.

So she ran along the River Wear
and stopped at the Boathouse to have a beer.
She sat for a while and wondered where to go,
then decided to go to the Gala to see a show.

But the Gala was closed so she walked to the
Market Place,
where there were lots of pigeons that she could
chase!
Something else important was there of course.
The famous Durham statue of a Man on a
Horse!

She thought she would pop to Milburngate,
but the sky grew dark and it was getting late.
She didn't know how to get back home,
she looked to the sky and gave a great moan.

The dog sat down and started to whine,
for her family she started to pine.
There was no-one on whom she could depend
oh, if only she had found a friend.

When all of a sudden a small boy sat down beside
her
and gently stroked her soft brown fur.
He said, "I'm so bored now, I just want to go home,
I am tired of sitting here on my own".

My family are shopping, they've spent lots of cash
and my sister is running in the Durham Dash.
The boy looked at the dog, the dog looked at him
and he couldn't be sure but the boy thought he saw the
dog grin.

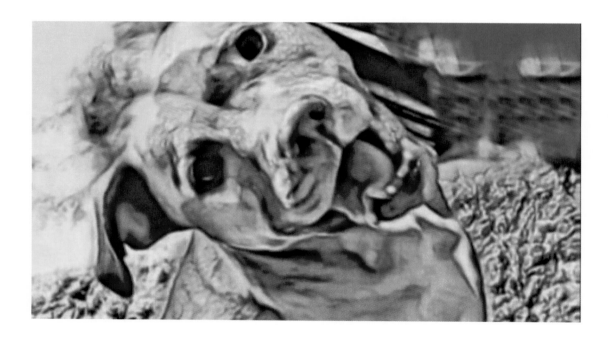

"Wait a minute, I know you", he said,
and it looked like the dog nodded her head!
"You live down my street, do you want to go
home?
You shouldn't be out here at night all alone."

17

"My parents will be waiting for me in our car.
Let's walk there together, it isn't that far."
So they walked to The Prince Bishops car park
and the dog was so happy she started to bark.

As they drove all the way to their street,
the dog watched the boy tapping his feet.
She wanted this boy to become her friend
but she had no money that she could spend.

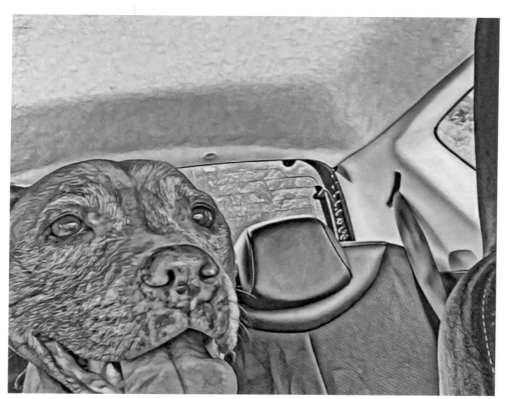

This young boy had been selfless and kind
and the dog knew he was one of a kind.
She wanted to show him how much she cared,
so went and found her favourite teddy bear.

She knew it wasn't much, but it was all that she had
and she hoped upon hope it would make the boy
glad.
She took the teddy and gave it to the boy,
even though it was her most favourite toy.

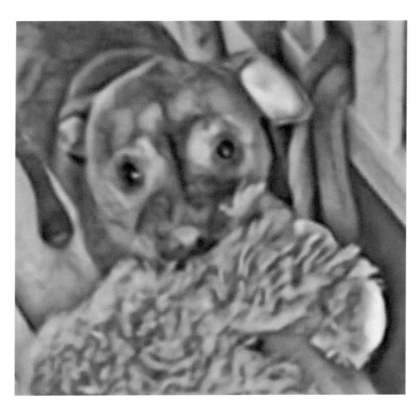

The boy stood and stared at the teddy at his feet
and he thought that this gift was extremely sweet,
for the dog to give to him her most favourite thing
and made him feel so important, it made him feel
like a king.

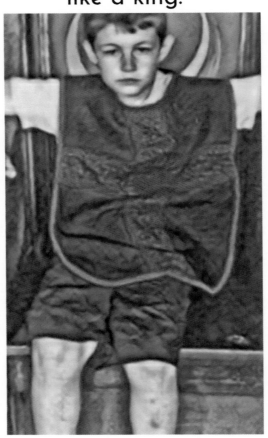

The boy was so happy to get the toy,
he leaped in the air and jumped for joy.
Then he crouched down beside the dog and sat
and she put her paw on his hand and gave it a pat.

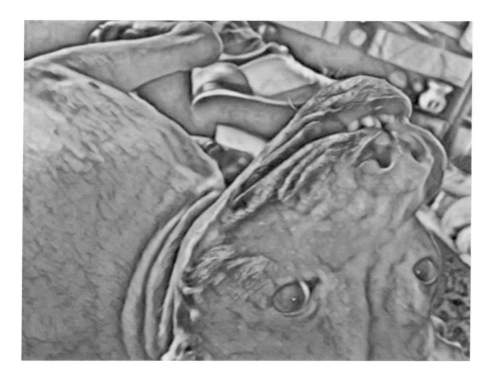

They had both finally made a friend,
they both thought about all the time they would
spend,
playing games together and all the things they
would do.
Except for the bit where the boy had to pick up her
poo!

The dog in the story is Holly, a Staffordshire Bull Terrier. Holly was adopted from kennels and found her forever home in 2014 with Catherine and her family. Holly is now 12 years old. Holly recently had a stroke but still loves to walk (a little slower!) around Durham Riverbanks and say hello to everyone! Maybe one day you might see Holly walking around Durham!

Also by Catherine Pugh

Available at Amazon.co.uk

Catherine is a qualified UK Primary school teacher and English as a Second Language Teacher. She lives in Durham with her partner, two teenage boys and Holly.

Contact Catherine

@authorcatherinepugh

@Catherine Pugh Author

@Catheri84421943

Hollydogwork@gmail.com

How many places have you been to?

The Man on the Horse statue ☐

The Market Place ☐

The Boathouse ☐

The Prince Bishops Shopping Centre ☐

Durham Castle ☐

Durham cathedral ☐

Palace Green ☐

The Gates ☐

Discover Durham ☐

The Gala Theatre ☐

What do you think makes a good friend?

_____

_____

_____

_____

_____

_____

_____

_____

_____

Draw a picture of your favourite pet animal

Printed in Great Britain
by Amazon